The Wild Adventures of

Eli Johnson & Curly Bill

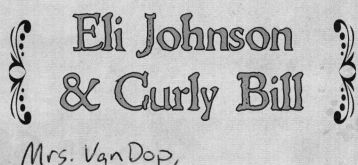

Mrs. VanDop,

Go have your own
Wild Adventures!

Dan Wright

DAN WRIGHT AND BILL WRIGHT
ILLUSTRATIONS BY SCOTT VANENGEN

DEDICATION

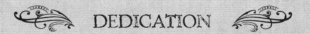

This book is dedicated to the many family and friends who helped shape my life and encourage me to continue writing this book. I want to personally thank my dad and mom for their constant support. I would also like to thank my wife for giving me the time and encouragement to press on when times got tough. This book is also dedicated to my sister Amy and my wonderful nieces and nephews. Finally, I want to dedicate this book to the memory of my beautiful sister Julie who was tragically taken from this earth. May her soul rest in peace in Heaven until the rest of our family meets her there.

FOREWORD: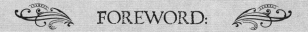

Never in my wildest dreams did I ever believe I would someday be involved in writing a book for others to read. This story was inspired by the tales my father told in his classroom. I finally grew sick of my friends, who graduated years ago, asking me if my dad still told the stories that they heard when they had him for a teacher. I knew that the time had come for these stories to be collected and put in book format so that others who may not have had the chance to hear the stories could finally read them, as well as let those who remember and love the stories to be able to relive them for years to come. I have had a blast working with my father on this project and I hope you enjoy reading it as much as I enjoyed putting it together.

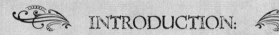

INTRODUCTION:

Our story begins in the territory of Colorado in a small town called Dustbowl. In mid-1800s America, towns along the Oregon-California Trail were nothing more than brief stops for travelers who were journeying out west in search of gold. Other people traveled west to start small general stores to service the many travelers along their journey. Whatever the reason for their travels, prospectors had much to fear on the journey, for danger lurked around every twist and turn of the trail.

Chapter 1:

Eighteen-year-old Eli Johnson decided to leave the East Coast and head west in search of a better life. It had been two years since the tragic loss of his father and mother in an accidental house fire, and Eli had grown tired of the loneliness that now plagued him. Eli became obsessed with his town's newspaper's stories of men and women striking it rich finding gold in the mountain and streams of California. After reading the newspaper one day, Eli decided to pack everything he owned on his horse named Scout and set off looking for new adventures.

Eli had set off from the East Coast months earlier when the traveling was fairly easy, but the trail soon grew dangerous and thin. Many travelers had met their end on this particular trail, for there were many dangers to be wary of. The farther he went west, the harder the trail was to follow. Every now and then he would pass through small towns and see different groups of people riding along in wagon trains. Conversation was little to none because strangers could not be trusted. Eli always kept his dog, Rex, by his side for protection. Though he was now very old, Rex was Eli's constant guardian as well as his only friend.

As he neared Dustbowl, Eli noticed this particular town had very few buildings—an old abandoned jail, a general store, and a hotel saloon dominated the landscape. Eli and Rex had been traveling for days and were exhausted when they finally arrived in the little town located within the untamed mountains of Colorado.

Eli booked a room in the small hotel saloon, asking the clerk if it was all right for Rex to share the room with him. The clerk assured him that it was okay, and Eli thanked him as he paid for his night's stay. As Eli sat in his room he looked at his faithful companion and said, "We're almost out of money, old boy. I don't think we even have enough to make it to the next town." Pulling his money bag from his belt, he counted off enough coins to buy a meal and put the rest back in the bag. Not one to worry about the future, Eli kicked off his cowboy boots and laid down for a nap.

Chapter 2:

That night a hungry Eli ventured down to the saloon to get some supper. He seated himself at an empty table just inside the saloon doors. The bar maid, who was about Eli's age, poured him a cool drink. "Hi, there," she began. "You look mighty hungry. I'll bring you a bowl of stew and some bread if you like."

"Yes. Stew sounds real good," Eli replied. In moments the young woman returned, and placing his meal on the table, she looked right at him and smiled. Eli noticed she was unusually pretty, and her blue eyes sparkled against the smoky atmosphere of the saloon.

"Is there anything more I can get you, Mr...?" She paused, waiting for Eli to tell her his name.

"The name's Eli," he blushed. "And I think I have all I need right here."

"Okay," she winked. "My name's Millie and I'll be right over by the bar if you need anything."

While Eli sat eating alone, he noticed a group of burly men playing cards at another table across the poorly lit room. The men were chewing and spitting tobacco into a spittoon on the floor. He noticed that every now and then the table would erupt in a fight that would result in a flurry of fists, cards, and curse words, sending shivers down the young man's spine.

Night after night Eli ate his meal in the saloon, which was always filled with a mixture of regulars and newcomers. The saloon was very lively, for everyone wanted to share the tales of adventures they had experienced while traveling along the trails. Eli particularly liked the stories about the wildlife that was said to roam around these parts. He hoped that someday he would see a mighty grizzly bear like the ones he heard about in the stories the men and women told. Unfortunately, stories of robbery, murder, and travelers being attacked by Indians were also a common theme around the saloon.

One night Eli ordered chicken and potatoes and was eating them when a couple of men from the bar began arguing over the price of a beaver hide. Eli had gotten so used to the constant fighting that he didn't even raise his head to see what it was about.

All of a sudden the two men came crashing into Eli's table. As Eli picked pieces of chicken out of his hair, he caught a quick glimpse of the champion of the skirmish. Standing around six feet three inches tall, a giant, curly headed man dusted himself off and headed back to the bar without apologizing to Eli for ruining his meal. Eli had not seen this particular man before and decided that it was best not to say anything to him about his ruined meal.

Chapter 3:

Eli picked himself up and quickly moved to the only available table, which happened to be the one right next to the poker game. He kept an eye on the table as he ordered another meal, and then a thought occurred to him. Maybe he could gain the money he needed to finish his trip to California by winning a few hands in poker. Eli knew the game well because he had often watched his father and his friend play poker at night at his house. The men at the table seemed more interested in chewing tobacco and trading stories than concentrating on the game. *I think I could win a few hands from these guys*, Eli thought.

After he had finished his meal he went over and stood by the table, just watching the game because there wasn't an open chair. A group of travelers also gathered around the table to watch the game because the table had grown quite rowdy as the participants began taunting each other. There were five players sitting at the table, four of them regulars, but one man had a face he had never seen before. After another hand was dealt, the newcomer at the table threw his cards down and yelled, "All right, I can't take it anymore, which one of ya is cheatin'?" He pulled out a six-shooter to reinforce his point.

The entire saloon went quiet as the men around the table studied the wide-eyed man. After a few seconds of silence, one of the men with a scar on his face let out a low chuckle. As his chuckle grew louder the others at the table joined in. "Are you blaming us for cheatin'?"

Out of the corner of his eye, Eli saw one of the men slowly pull out a giant bowie knife from his boot underneath the table. Eli could see that all of the men around the table were enormous brutes who had lived off the land their entire lives. A majority of them were trappers who bore the scars of one too many skirmishes with the Indians in the surrounding areas. Each man was equipped with a six-shooter pistol permanently strapped to his hip.

Quick as a whip, the man with the knife jumped up and sliced the gun-toting stranger's hand. His pistol and bits of flesh hit the table as he screamed in agony. The man with the scar lunged on the table and grabbed the fallen pistol and held it to the injured man's temple. "Mister," he said, "how would you like to be shot with your own weapon?"

The man began to stammer, "N-No, sir. I'm sorry."

"Then you better apologize to me and the boys for callin' us cheaters. You see, we're nice gentlemen," his lips cracking open to a mocking smile, "and we don't cheat."

"Sir, I'm s-sorry I called you cheaters. If I can just get my weapon, I'll leave and never return."

The man holding the gun cracked the chamber open and the sound of bullets hitting the floor could be heard throughout the saloon. "Here ya go."

When the frightened man saw this, he blurted, "But I'll never survive out there without ammunition. There are wolves and bears and Indians. I'm as good as dead."

"I guess I could put them back in the gun," the man said with an evil glint in his eye.

Knowing the man with the scar would shoot him if he told him to put the bullets back in the gun, the terrified victim stammered, "No, I-I'll take my chances in the forest."

And just like that the man sprinted out the saloon's doors, causing them to flap back and forth violently. Slowly the saloon came back to life.

Eli spotted the open chair left vacant by the man, but thought, *do I dare sit there?* But being young and reckless, Eli quickly put all reason out of his mind. Eli blurted out, "You got an open chair, I see. Can I get in on the next hand?"

Chapter 4:

Admiring his newly won pistol, the man with the scar replied, "Sure, kid, have a seat." Eli sat down and took out his bag of coins. Excited at the chance to play with the men, Eli took the momentary break in the game to look at the activities around the table. As Eli looked around, he noticed the dealer was playing cards with one hand since he was missing his other one—and that he was pretty good at it too. He would shuffle the cards with his only hand, put them in his mouth, and spit them out to the men around the table. Eli could hardly believe his eyes!

Eli picked up the hand he had been dealt. He started to admire his lucky hand then realized the cards were covered in tobacco juice. He decided that he should turn his attention elsewhere.

"I'd like to introduce myself. My name is Eli Johnson," said Eli. As he was introducing himself he looked in the direction of a man who had fang marks up and down his arm. The man looked like he hadn't shaved in days, and his hair was grimy from weeks without a bath. He wore a permanent scowl on his lips as he said,

"They call me Rattlesnake."

"How did you get a name like that?" Eli asked, stunned.

"Don't ever ask me that again," hissed Rattlesnake.

Startled by the man's rudeness, Eli turned his attention to the one-armed dealer. Smiling, his teeth black as night, the dealer said, "They call me One Arm Jack."

"Well, I won't ask you why," said Eli.

"Go ahead and ask me. I'd love to tell ya."

"Okay, how did it happen?" asked Eli curiously.

"Don't ever ask me again!" bellowed the man.

Eli about fell over. "But...but you just told me to."

"Ha (cough) ha (cough)," One Arm Jack chuckled the best he could. "Just kiddin' ya, son, let me tell you how it happened. I was up trappin' in Canada one time, bent over to check my trap, when I heard heavy breathing behind me. I didn't have a darn clue what it was. Slowly I reached for my six-shooter. Before I knew what happened my arm was in the mouth of the biggest grizzly bear I'd ever seen! That old bear bit down so hard he clean cut my arm off! Off ran that grizzly, and when I looked up, I saw my arm bouncing up and down as if wavin' me good-bye."

At that the old trapper started laughing. Eli had to admit that was pretty funny. The next man at the table, the one with the scar on his face, spoke up right away, not to be outdone. "Son, they call me Horseshoe. You can probably see why." Horseshoe pointed to an imprint of a shoe on his face. "My old horse kicked me right here, broke my cheekbone and my jaw. But ask me what I did to the horse," he chuckled. "I ate him!"

The next guy told Eli to mind his own business and play cards. Old One Arm Jack could deal cards with his one hand as fast as any man with two. Around the cards went again. Eli picked up his. Discovering he had a perfect hand, Eli flipped a silver dollar in the air, landing it in the center of the table. "I'll raise."

As the men went around the table betting, Eli knew he had them beat. Eli was stunned as old Rattlesnake looked at him and grunted, "I call ya, boy." They laid their cards down, and Eli couldn't believe what he saw. Rattlesnake had the winning hand.

"Wait a minute," Eli protested.

One Arm Jack looked at him with a menacing look and said, "You doubtin' him, boy?"

Eli quickly backed down. "I don't want any trouble," he said. The next hand was dealt, same result. Eli had good hands, but he lost every one.

About that time he noticed that another group of people had gathered around the table. One of the men in the crowd, the man who had fought at Eli's table, made eye contact with Eli and motioned him with his eyes to look at Rattlesnake and One Arm Jack. Then he nodded toward Horseshoe, as if to tell Eli that the guys were up to something.

Eli said, "Men, deal me out this hand, I gotta use the outhouse." He got up and excused himself from the table. Eli noticed the curly headed man go outside. Once out of the sight of the men at the table, Eli followed him.

Chapter 5:

"What are you trying to tell me?" he asked.

The man looked around and whispered," The name's Curly Bill, and those men have been cheatin'. Old One Arm Jack's got an extra deck under the table, and he's handin' cards to Horseshoe and Rattlesnake. That's why you're losin' your money."

Eli countered defiantly, "No one cheats me. They're going to pay for this."

Curly Bill was quick to answer, "Careful, boy, they're wanted all over Canada for illegal trappin' and murder. They're bandits, all right, but they won't let you get away with any smart talk. If I were you I'd call it a night."

But Eli was too mad to listen to Curly Bill's advice and stormed back into the saloon determined to get even with the cheating men.

As Eli sat down, he silently took out his six-shooter and set it on his lap. The table covered his six-shooter well, and he figured if worse came to worst he could shoot any of the men in the belly. A couple of those big bellies would be hard to miss, he thought. Eli looked each man in the eye and said, "Deal 'em."

So One Arm Jack started dealing around the table. Eli picked up his cards. It was another great hand.

Rattlesnake read Eli's face right away and said, "Put your cards on the table. I call ya." Eli took all of his coins and slapped them down. Old Horseshoe glanced over at One Arm Jack. About that time, Eli saw Old Jack's one arm slip under the table. Eli's hand also went under the table.

As quick as a lightning striking on the prairie, Eli sprang up, six-shooter trained directly on One Arm Jack. With clenched teeth Eli muttered, "I know you're cheatin' and I intend to do something about it." Before Eli could get the threat out of his mouth, Old Horseshoe whipped out his six-shooter as fast as any man could and put it to Eli's head.

"Boy, no one calls my friend One Arm Jack a cheater and lives to tell about it."

Chapter 6:

At that very moment, Horseshoe heard the hammer of a six-shooter being pulled back right behind his own head. "That will be quite enough," Curly Bill said in a shrewd tone. "I reckon you should give the boy back his money." Horseshoe turned around to find the barrel of a six-shooter pointed right between his eyes.

Eli laughed. "Sir, kindly put your weapon on the table." Eli's hand went back to his six-shooter as he gave One Arm Jack his orders. "Ease your weapon up."

Several people around the table fled in panic seeing that nothing good was going to come from this situation. "Thank you, men," smiled Eli. "Now I'm going to take my money back, and I'm going to take yours too, because I probably would've won it anyway." He reached over and pulled all the money toward him.

Curly Bill went around the table gathering each man's gun and then emptied the bullets onto the ground. Eli motioned to the now terrified bar maid to bring him something to carry the money in. Quickly she brought him a cloth bag, and he scooped the pile of coins into it. It was heavy; there was enough money in that bag for two men to live on for an entire year. Without thinking, Eli leaned forward and kissed the frightened young woman on the cheek. "Thank you for your help, miss," he said with a wink.

By now Rattlesnake was foaming at the mouth with anger, fire was flaring up in Horseshoe's eye, and One Arm Jack's one arm was just a-shakin'.

Rattlesnake reached down into his cowboy boot and grabbed his bowie knife. Rattlesnake was a champion with that knife. One flick of his wrist and he could stick a flying butterfly to the wall. Rattlesnake continued to pull the knife out ever so slowly.

Out of the corner of his eye, Eli saw Rattlesnake take out the knife and attempt to stab Curly Bill. Eli reached over and flipped the table, knocking the three men onto their backs. When Rattlesnake fell backwards, the bowie knife left his hand and went twisting in the air and came straight down, pinning his ear to the floor. As Rattlesnake screamed in pain, Eli yelled, "Curly Bill, let's get outta here!"

Eli and Curly Bill took off toward the old hinged saloon doors. Rattlesnake hollered after them, "I'm gonna make you pay for this if it's the last thing I do!" The two men jumped on their horses without even putting their feet in the stirrups, and away they rode. Eli let out a loud whistle and Rex came crashing through the second-story window of his hotel room onto the roof and then down to the ground after them.

Chapter 7:

"Yah, yah!" they yelled as dust kicked up around them.

Now it was about two o'clock in the morning, and it was very dark. The night was so black that the men could not see the trail, so they loosened their grip on the reins and let the horses guide the way. They ran and ran. Both men could hear old Rex panting as he struggled to keep up with the horses. For what seemed like hours they fled before letting up their gallop. For a moment the men could only hear the sound of the horses' heartbeats racing and old Rex panting. The men listened for other sounds as the silence overwhelmed them.

Curly Bill jumped off his horse and put his ear to the ground. He listened for the thunder of their enemies' horses' hooves. He did not hear a thing. After a couple of tense moments, Curly Bill stood. "You know what? I think we lost them. They're probably on the trail now, and they're going to track us. You can count on it. Like I said back at the saloon, these men are wanted for all kinds of dastardly deeds."

Both men, relieved they had bought some time, got back on their horses while Rex trotted a few feet behind them. At last, Curly Bill sighed, "Looks like we can ride a little easier now. Tell me a little bit about yourself, Eli. Why are you out in these parts?"

Eli started, "I come from Virginia and am headin' out west to make a fortune in—"

Before Eli could finish his sentence Curly Bill stopped him. "Virginia? I was raised in West Virginia. We're practically neighbors." Right away the two men hit it off and became the best of friends.

"Curly Bill," Eli got real serious and looked his comrade in the eyes, "I gotta thank you for what you did back there in that saloon."

"Anytime, my friend. You do plan on sharing that bag of money, don't you?"

Eli laughed, "That's the least I can do for you saving my life."

The two men rode on. It was nearly four in the morning when they grew too tired to ride any farther. They agreed on a spot a little off the trail where they tied up their horses and built a small fire. In one of his saddlebags Eli had some food and a jar for water. Eli went down to the stream next to their camp and filled it up with fresh water. Before long they were sitting around a campfire eating, drinking, and sharing stories. "I'm tired," Eli finally confessed as he took his saddle down from Scout's back and made himself a pillow.

"Well, who's going to keep watch?" Curly Bill asked.

"No need to worry, I've got the best watchdog in the world," Eli boasted. "Ain't nobody going to sneak up on us with Rex around."

Curly Bill laughed at the young man's arrogance and said, "He's a good dog for sure, but I think I'll keep watch too." Curly Bill looked on as Eli fell sound asleep, his faithful dog guarding him by his side. He gazed worriedly into the fire. He knew the reputation those men back at the saloon had, and they would stop at nothing to get their revenge. But soon even these thoughts were eclipsed by the flickering fire, and Curly Bill fell into a deep sleep.

Chapter 8:

Around sunup the men were awakened by the sound of Rex growling. Immediately both reached for their six-shooters. Old Rex's hair was standing on end, and he was pointed in the direction of the woods. "What is it, Rex?" Eli whispered. Rex continued growling, his ears fully alert and every hair on his neck standing razor sharp on edge. Eli turned to Curly Bill, "We got trouble on our hands."

Rex started bellowing as loud as he could, and both men, six-shooters drawn, stood ready to do battle. Rex went between Eli's legs, shaking. *I've never seen Rex act like this*, thought Eli. "Rex, what's the matter? Go get 'em, boy."

But the dog wouldn't move. Then all of a sudden he ran to the edge of the woods and started barking again. The men crept up to see what he was looking at, but as they came near the dog, Rex turned and bolted straight toward camp. The spooked dog ran right by Eli and Curly Bill and sat down by the fire. The men were shaken but continued to approach the edge of the woods, six-shooters trained on whatever was lurking behind the thick brush. Cautiously they entered, but Curly Bill became ensnared in a thicket of prickly thorns.

Eli continued on, not knowing his comrade was no longer with him. Something large rustled in the brush nearby, but the trees were so thick he could not see what it was. Eli turned in the direction of the noise just in time to see a massive grizzly bear spring from the bushes. As he looked at the enormous grizzly, it let out a deafening roar.

The bear stood on its hind legs, saliva dripped from its mouth, evil permeating from his beady yellow eyes. In an instant, a paw came down and knocked the revolver out of Eli's hand. Helpless, Eli watched the pistol fall in slow motion to the mossy forest floor. The bear swatted again knocking Eli to the ground. Eli could feel blood trickle from his forehead as he tried to get back on his feet. Eli stared up into the jaws of the mighty grizzly and prepared for the worst.

Like a flash of lightning, Rex came out of the bushes and grabbed hold of the bear's throat. The massive animal roared angrily and rose back up on hind feet. Standing at least nine feet tall, the grizzly swung Rex violently back and forth in the air, trying to loosen the dog's grip. But Rex had a death grip on the bear's throat, and he refused to let go. At last the growling bear was able to sink his razor sharp claws into the side of the dog. Rex howled in pain as he fell limp to the ground. He lay helpless, blood oozing from his pierced ribs. His entire body was paralyzed except his head. Struggling against the pain, the wounded dog lifted his head as if to tell Eli to run.

But Eli did not listen to his friend's advice and dove for his six-shooter and unloaded several shots in the direction of the bear. One of the bullets penetrated the bear's eye socket, leaving the bear with one good eye. Seemingly unfazed by the bullets, the bear again advanced toward Eli. Before the grizzly could reach him, another round of bullets came from behind Eli. Curly Bill had managed to free himself from the thorn bushes and had rushed to the aid of his friend. As Curly Bill continued to fire off shots from his six-shooter, the bear, realizing he could not defeat the men and their guns, let out a final mighty roar and dove headlong into the bushes, leaving a trail of blood behind him.

With the bear gone, Eli immediately dropped on top of the fallen dog and started sobbing uncontrollably. Placing his hand on his friend's back, Curly Bill tried to console him. "There's nothing you can do for him now." Eli ignored Curly Bill and continued stroking the bloody dog's head. After a few moments Curly Bill said, "We have to put him out of his misery, Eli, he's in too much pain right now and we have no way of fixing his injuries."

Eli knew Curly Bill was right. He turned to Curly Bill and muttered, "I'd like to have a moment alone with my dog."

"I understand." With those words Curly Bill turned to leave. "When you've said your good-byes, if you want, I'll come back and put the dog to rest. With tears in his eyes Eli nodded okay. As soon as Curly Bill stepped out of the bushes he heard a loud shot. He dropped his head and said a quick prayer. Rex had laid down his life for Eli. Now Eli had done the best thing he could do for his friend. This turn of events was not fair, but Curly Bill knew nothing on this trail really was. From now on the two men had to have each other's back if they wanted to survive; there was no one else to help them.

Nearly two hours later, Eli emerged from the woods and approached the smoldering fire. He told Curly Bill that he had covered Rex with large stones. It would be a memorial for all those who would come after them to remember the sacrifice that Rex made for his friends. Both men agreed that it was now time for them to get back on the trail as they suspected the men from the saloon were still following them.

As Curly Bill mounted his horse, Eli stopped. He turned and gazed toward the resting place of his beloved dog and said, "I'm going to miss you, boy. There will never be another one like you." With that he mounted his horse, unaware that a single yellow eye watched them leave.

Chapter 9:

The two men rode in silence for hours. Each man kept thinking about the events that had unfolded in the past twenty-four hours. Finally Eli broke the silence. "You know, I got this funny feeling we're being followed. Every now and then I'll look behind me and see something peering out of the shadows. I can't tell if it's a man, animal, or just the shadow of a tree branch. I don't know if I'm seeing things, but I'll tell you what. You keep riding, and I'm going to stay behind this rock. You take my horse with you; if someone followed us they'll think I'm with ya. If it's Rattlesnake, Horseshoe, and One Arm Jack, I'll take care of them."

And just like that Eli hopped off his horse and somersaulted behind the rock. Curly Bill grabbed Scout's reins and gave a final look back to where Eli was hiding. He could see the young man slowly reloading his six-shooter. Before Curly Bill rounded a corner in the trail he yelled back at his friend, "I'll go an hour up a head and then I'll make camp. Stay safe, my friend."

Eli settled in next to the rock he was hiding behind. He could see the trail and felt he had a perfect position to ambush anyone who was tracking them. As he pressed his back against the boulder, he told himself to stay alert. He was very tired because he had not gotten a good night's rest since the activities at the saloon. As the hours ticked on by, Eli's eyes grew heavy. Every now and then he would wipe his eyes, shake his head, and convince himself he was wide awake. Before he knew it, he had fallen sound asleep.

Click! Eli jolted awake, realizing that he dozed off. As he groggily lifted his cowboy hat off his face he felt the presence of a cold object pressed against his temple. Eli instantly knew it was the barrel of a six-shooter. The sound that had awaken him was the hammer being pulled back on the gun that was now boring deeply into his temple.

Eli was now wide awake. He slowly turned his head in the direction of the one who held the gun. As Eli's eyes drifted up the man's body he noticed that the man only had one arm.

Chapter 10:

"Ha (cough) ha (cough), so we meet again," the man snickered. "Let me reintroduce myself. My name is One Arm Jack." Out from behind the boulder stepped two more men. "And you remember my friends, don't ya, Rattlesnake and Horseshoe."

Old Rattlesnake had a mouth full of chewing tobacco from which he spit a giant wad right in Eli's eye. Eli cried out in pain at the stinging sensation, and as he wiped the tobacco out of his eye he lunged at Rattlesnake to get his revenge. But One Arm Jack was too quick and brought the butt of his six-shooter down squarely on Eli's head. Eli dropped to the ground as blackness rushed into his vision.

Chapter 11:

The sound of a vulture's squawking overhead brought Eli out of the unconsciousness caused by his concussion. It sat directly above Eli as if to tell the other birds circling overhead that Eli was his meal. Eli began to panic but could not move because his hands were bound tightly behind him. In fact, his whole body was bound tightly against a tree. As he began to contemplate how he could escape, he smelled something sweet coming from his body. Eli knew he had smelled the odor before, but because he was tied so tightly, he could not look down to see what it was. After a few minutes of squirming, he reached out with his tongue and tasted the sticky substance. As soon as Eli's tongue hit the substance his heart sank; it was honey!

Eli struggled hard against the rope trying to break free. The ropes would not loosen, and Eli's worst fears were now realized. The three bandits, having used an old Indian trick of tying up their victim, coating them with honey, and leaving them smack dab in the middle of bear country, were now nowhere to be found. Eli knew it was just a matter of time before a bear, possibly the giant grizzly they had just fought, would pick up on the smell of the honey and make a beeline straight for Eli. Eli had heard from other travelers at the saloon that grizzlies were known for having powerful noses that could pick up the scent of food from miles away.

Crack, crack! A shiver went right down Eli's spine when he heard twigs being crushed behind him. Eli heard the sound of heavy breathing. Something big was approaching from behind. He tried to turn to see what it was but the ropes held him firmly to the tree. That something was now ten feet behind him.

Eli wiggled more desperately trying to get out, but the ropes held tight and burned into his skin. Eli's body went limp with fear as he smelled the awful stink of hot animal breath upon his neck. He tried to think clearly as the animal sniffed him from behind. Eli remembered that his father had taught him years ago that a man's best option against a hungry grizzly bear was to play dead. Unfortunately his father had also told him that if it was a black bear this trick would not work because black bears typically do not care if their food is alive or dead. The only option was to stand your ground and fight the bear.

With his current situation in mind, Eli prayed that it was a grizzly. As the animal continued to sniff the back of his head, Eli tried to be as stiff as possible. He could only hope his heart, which was beating loudly, would not give him away.

The animal slowly came around to the front of the tree. Not wanting to see what it was, Eli Johnson closed his eyes in fear. His entire journey flashed before him. He had survived so many events so far, but it seemed to him that this was the end of the trail.

Eli felt the animal rise up on its hind legs. Realizing that there was nothing left for him to do, Eli tensed up as he waited for the bear to bite down...

Chapter 12:

The beast's breath was now blowing directly in Eli's face. With his eyes closed, Eli pictured a huge bear. As his mind began to function again, Eli suddenly realized that the breeze was blowing from behind him, away from him. He wondered, *If the bear smelled the honey from afar, wouldn't it have approached me from the front instead of from the rear?* Curiosity finally got the best of Eli and he flung his eyes open to face his assailant.

"Hee haw, hee haw!" A startled mule jumped back as Eli opened his eyes. After recovering from the shock, the mule advanced toward Eli again, hoping to get another taste of the delicious honey coating his body. Eli started to crack a smile when he heard another sound behind him.

"Hee hee, how ya doing partner?" Eli looked up to see a man. It was a toothless man. No teeth whatsoever. The man hobbled over to Eli and studied him for a moment. "Kind of in a predicament, ain't ya?" Every time the man talked, spit flew out and hit Eli in the face. The man was short—and very old. Eli could see that he walked with a limp.

"Hi ya, I'd be Miner Mike. That's what they call me, Miner Mike. Yup, yup, yup, yup, that's what they call me." Before Miner Mike could say another word, the mule knocked him aside and let out another "Hee haw, hee haw" right in Eli's face and began to lick the honey off of him.

Miner Mike cackled. Hee hee hee, I see you met my mule, Sal. Yup, that's Sal. I think Sal likes you." At that Sal stopped eating the honey and gave Eli a wet mule kiss! That was the last straw for Eli.

"Yuck!" Eli yelled while trying to spit hair out of his mouth. "Are you going to get me out of this or are you going to let your mule lick me to death?"

"Te… Tell…Tell me something, what are you doing in my part of the woods?" the old man asked as his voice got real soft. Then an angry look came over his face, and Miner Mike reached down into his boot and pulled out a giant bowie knife and pointed it directly at Eli. Eli started to panic, wishing a bear would have attacked him from the back instead of having this crazy old toothless man stab him with his bowie knife.

Chapter 13:

Miner Mike took a step toward him and looked Eli directly in the eye and said, "You're kind of scared of me, ain't ya, ha ha ha. I'm only gonna loosen the ropes, yup, that's what I'm gonna do."

Miner Mike reached around the tree and cut the ropes that bound Eli to the tree. Eli let out a sigh of relief as he rubbed his hands, which hurt from being tied so tight. Eli reached out to pet Sal as she continued to clean the honey off of him. Sal reached her head up around Eli's chest and nuzzled Miner Mike. She looked to be as old as Miner Mike himself. Eli watched the two interact and it seemed to him that the two acted like they were husband and wife. Old Sal had all of the pots and pans Miner Mike owned attached to her saddle. As Eli began to thank Miner Mike for saving his life, he was interrupted by the sound of pots and pans clanging together as Sal went running off into the woods.

Miner Mike's face went from happy to startled as he chased after his old mule yelling, "Sal, you stop this instant, you hear me? You...you come back right now!" Eli chuckled as the sight of Miner Mike hobbling after the old mule as they disappeared around a bend in the trail. Eli wished he could have had a chance to properly thank Miner Mike, but he had a funny feeling that he would be seeing the old man again.

Eli took a deep breath; *I wonder where the three bandits went?* Judging by the position of the sun, he could tell it had not been too long since their run-in. Curly Bill had taken Eli's horse and the bandits had taken his six-shooter, leaving him defenseless against predators. He decided that the only thing he could do was start walking to where Curly Bill was camped.

Chapter 14:

Eli got back on the trail and started walking. He could see the hoof prints of three horses that he assumed belonged to Horseshoe, Rattlesnake, and One Arm Jack. Eli tried to follow the tracks the best he could, but the sun had begun to set, making it hard to follow them. As he kept walking he thought, *I sure hope Curly Bill doesn't come back for me, because if he does, he'll run directly into the three outlaws.*

After walking for an hour or so, he started to hear voices coming from farther up the trail. Eli crept up close to where the voices were coming from, careful not to make a noise that would give away his position. He did not know what he would do when he found the men, for he didn't have a weapon to attack them with. He came within seeing distance of the camp and spotted the men sitting around the campfire. He could hear their conversation and smell the food they were cooking over the fire.

He crouched behind a tree and waited till, slowly, all three men drifted off to sleep. Eli crept into the bandit's camp, approaching it with caution. A smile appeared on Eli's face as he thought how easy it would be to end the bandits' lives in revenge for all the trouble they had caused. They had wanted to do the same to him, why shouldn't he return the favor?

Before he could make his move, the voice of his father rang in his head, "Do unto others as you would have them do to you." Eli remembered his father's words fondly and thought, *I don't want to be like these men, running from place to place, ducking the authorities. I have a different idea.*

Chapter 15:

Like most cowboys in those days, the outlaws slept with their six-shooters by their sides. Their hands were permanently fixed on them because on these trails a man never knew when he might need it. Eli looked around and spotted his six-shooter hanging out of one of the saddlebags, directly under the head of Rattlesnake. Eli stopped and shuddered. Rattlesnake was an enormous man who could take out Eli with just one hand if he had the chance. Eli knew that he had to be extremely cautious if he wanted to get out of the situation alive.

He crept up as quiet as he could right next to Rattlesnake. "Zzzzzzzzzzzzzzzzzzzzzzzzsnort snort oink!!!" Rattlesnake let out a loud snore, rolled over, faced in Eli's direction, and continued sleeping. Startled, Eli reached out slowly to grab his six-shooter. His hand was within inches of the butt of the gun when One Arm Jack sat straight up and looked right at Eli!

Eli froze as his heart leapt into his mouth. His eyes met One Arm Jack's but he saw at once that they were glassed over. As he watched, One Arm Jack got up and started to walk; Eli realized he was sleepwalking! One Arm Jack slowly started to lumber toward the trail, but there was a log directly in his path. Eli knew One Arm Jack would trip over that log, wake up, and alert the other two bandits of his presence.

Without thinking, Eli grabbed the six-shooter and took off for the brush, looking over his shoulder just in time to see One Arm Jack step over the log as if he was awake. With this stroke of luck, Eli changed his plans and hurried over to where the men's horses were tied up. Eli thought to himself, *If I set the horses free they can't follow me.*

As he neared the horses, they started to stomp their feet. "Shh, easy now." Eli tried to comfort the nervous horses. One of the horses started to whinny. Eli froze in place. As the horse whinnied again, One Arm Jack turned around and looked in the direction of Eli. Eli tried to stay as still as possible but the horse was spooked by Eli's presence and gave a final neigh.

Rattlesnake shot straight up out of his bed. "Hey, the horses!"

Eli took off running with the horses between him and the men. The outlaws tried to aim their guns at Eli but could not shoot him without hitting their horses. This made the men furious as they yelled curses and threats about what they would do to Eli if they caught him.

When Eli got a sizable distance away from the men he slapped the horses on the behind and they ran off in different directions into the woods. The men ran after Eli, but they were out of shape from too many nights of playing cards at the saloon. They gave up the chase and returned to camp swearing that they would find Eli in the morning.

Chapter 16:

Eli, out of breath himself, got back on the trail and continued his search for Curly Bill. It wasn't long before he smelled the smoke of another fire. As he got closer to the smoke he realized that this was Curly Bill's camp. Curly Bill was sound asleep with their two horses tied up next to him. Feeling good about his defeat of the bandits, Eli thought he would play a joke on Curly Bill. He crept up to where Curly Bill was sleeping and prepared to scare his friend by pretending to growl like a bear. Eli let out a mighty roar, but Curly Bill didn't move.

Eli whipped off the blankets to find a rock where Curly Bill's head should have been. At that moment, something behind him let out a giant roar! Eli jumped high in the air in fright before he heard the familiar sound of his friend laughing behind him.

When Curly Bill stopped laughing he asked, "What in the world is that smell? You smell like...like honey!"

Eli, trying hard not to laugh, said, "I may smell like that, but you better not call me honey."

And with that the two men started laughing again. Eli told Curly Bill the whole story of his escape. After listening, Curly Bill remarked, "We better get saddled up and on our way. I reckon those men will eventually find their horses and come looking for us." Curly Bill, who had traveled these trails before, recommended that the men take the river next to the trail so that their tracks could not be followed. So the men gathered their belongings and saddled their horses.

After traveling in the river for an hour, the men got back on the trail and continued riding. After riding in silence for a while Curly Bill spoke up. "I think we should take this trail till we reach Canada. There's a bounty on the heads of Horseshoe, Rattlesnake, and One Arm Jack for some trouble they caused during their time up there. We should be safe there because in Canada, they shoot first and ask questions second. Those men wouldn't dare cross the border after us." And with that, the two men went into a full gallop trying desperately to reach the border before the three bandits caught them.

Chapter 17:

As daylight broke the men crossed the Canadian border. Breathing hard, the horses went into a trot and the conversation turned into where the men should go from there. Curly Bill explained that he had spent the last five years in Canada earning a living by trapping and selling animal hides. He suggested that they could go to an uninhabited location he knew about where they could spend the winter trapping animals and in the spring return to Dustbowl and sell the furs they caught.

Eli thought that was a good idea. He asked Curly Bill, "I've heard the Indians that inhabit Canada are extremely hostile to the white man. Is that true?"

Curly Bill did not say anything right away, then carefully responded, "Many Indians have been taken advantage of by men like us. Before the white man invaded their lands, the Indians were a relatively peaceful people. I have personally seen Indians taken into slavery and some ruthlessly murdered. We must be on the lookout for danger, for the Indians in the area may mistake us as the men who wished to do them harm."

The two men stopped in a small town right across the border and went into a supply store. They took all the coins they had "inherited" back in Dustbowl and bought traps, cooking supplies, and enough flour, salt, and various other foods to get them through the winter. They also bought a pack mule to carry the supplies for them.

As they left the town, the trail became hard to follow because it was so overgrown with trees and brush. They crossed raging rivers with slippery stones on the bottom that made it impossible for them to ride their horses across. With each river the men came to, they had to dismount their horses and lead them across, hoping that they did not slip themselves and be carried off by the current. Wildlife was everywhere along the trail. The men saw countless bears and moose grazing in the many fields and swamps that littered the countryside. On one occasion, while crossing a river, they encountered a pack of wolves who were feeding upon an elk carcass. Having run into men and their guns before, the wolves ran at the sight of them. Eli, having never seen a wolf before, was transfixed by the haunting howls the wolves made as they scurried away from the men.

"Wolves' pelts bring a high price these days," Curly Bill whispered, "but we'll stick to trapping beaver, minks, pine martins, and otters. I just can't bring myself to kill such a majestic animal as the wolf no matter the bounty placed on their heads."

As the men watched the wolves disappear from sight, Eli began to understand the great respect Curly Bill had for the woods around them. Although he was not opposed to taking an animal life for survival or cutting down trees for shelter, Curly Bill would not tolerate the aimless destruction of life that so many men before them had participated in.

Chapter 18:

The men traveled along the trail for about a week, camping along the river. One morning Eli was awoken by the sound of an animal going through their food bag. He was about to go see what it was when Curly Bill stopped him.

"You don't want to go anywhere near that animal," he cautioned.

As Eli stood up to look at the animal he whispered, "What's the big deal? It looks like a small dog."

Curly Bill fired several shots in the air and the animal fled for the woods. "That, my friend, is a wolverine. The most vicious animal you'll meet in these parts. I once was out trapping when the horse I was ridin' was attacked by a wolverine. When it had killed my horse it came after me! Luckily it was no match for my six-shooter. There are many dangerous things in these woods; you'd do best to listen to my advice."

Finally the men arrived at the place in which they would make their home. Eli could see mountains off in the distance, but the land they were standing on was surrounded by smaller hills. As they walked farther they came upon the clearing where Curly Bill had built his cabin. The grass surrounding the cabin was long, for it was late August. The trees were full of leaves preventing the men from seeing far.

Behind the cabin was a tall hill that had a ridge running along the side of it. As Eli gazed up the hill he thought he saw something move. For the rest of the hike to Curly Bill's cabin Eli couldn't shake the feeling that something or someone was watching them.

Chapter 19:

Eli turned to Curly Bill and asked," Do you have the feeling that someone or something is watching us?"

Curly Bill responded, "Not only do I have the feeling, I *know* someone is watching us."

Eli was shocked at Curly Bill's response. "What are you talking about?"

"They've been following ever since the trail met the river. I didn't say anything to you because I didn't want them to know we knew they were there."

Eli said, "What are you talking about? Who's following us? Is it...One Arm Jack?"

"Slowly, carefully, turn around and look at the ridge," directed Curly Bill.

As Eli turned his head he saw three Indian braves seated on paint horses. Their long black hair flowed in the wind. They had the reins of the horses in one hand and deadly looking spears in the other. The braves sat on their horses wearing nothing but a loincloth, their tan skin smeared with bear grease. The braves rode without a saddle, for they preferred to feel closer to their horses. Each brave was equipped with a bow draped across his shoulder and a quiver full of arrows across his back.

As Eli's eyes met the braves he felt as if they ushered him a warning: "We will be watching you," and in an instant the Indians disappeared over the hill.

Before Eli could say a word, Curly Bill said, "Relax, my friend, they were just letting us know they're watching us. If they wanted to hurt us we would already be dead."

"Well, I don't like this situation, let's turn around and head back."

"And face One Arm Jack? By now they've found their horses and they outnumber us."

Eli knew Curly Bill had a point. Curly Bill took a moment to think then said, "I'll tell you what we'll do. Tomorrow we'll look the area over. If we find more Indians we'll head back."

Eli did not like Curly Bill's plan, but thought if Curly Bill wasn't scared then he shouldn't be either.

Chapter 20:

The men spent that night in Curly Bill's old cabin. It was very small, having only one room to sleep in, but was equipped with a tiny kitchen where a man could cook his meals and clean his furs. The next day they went up to the ridge to see if they could track the Indians. But the Indians were smart and had gone into the river to avoid being tracked, the same way Eli and Curly Bill had done to avoid the bandits.

Several more days passed with no sign of Indians in the area, so the men felt sure that they were safe.

After a few nights passed the men realized that the little cabin Curly Bill had built would not be big enough for them to live in, so they began to cut down trees in order to build a bigger cabin. The trees in the surrounding area were fairly thin so it didn't take long for the men to amass enough building materials to add on to the current cabin. By now it was early September and the leaves had begun to fall as winter approached. Week after week went by as the cabin started to take form.

Chapter 21:

One afternoon while the men were taking a break from the construction of their cabin they heard an abundance of clicking noises coming from outside. Eli had never heard a sound like this before, and when he turned to ask Curly Bill what it was, he noticed that Curly Bill was gone. Frightened, Eli ran out to the deck of the cabin to see Curly Bill staring out into the prairie in front of their cabin. As Eli gazed out to where Curly Bill was looking, he was amazed to see a peculiar looking deer-like animal with large horns running past. There were hundreds of them. After watching them for what seemed like forever, Eli whispered, "Wow, what kind of animal is that?"

Curly Bill took a sip of his coffee and responded, "Those, my friend, are caribou. Aren't they beautiful? Caribou migrate through these parts in the fall. The noise you hear is made because caribou have a loose tendon rolling around in their ankles that make a clicking noise every time they take a step."

Because of the size of the herd, the noise they made was almost deafening. As Curly Bill finished his coffee he said, "I think it's time we got our food for the winter."

The men raced inside and grabbed their rifles, purchased from the general store, and took a position about twenty yards from where the herd was. They could have closed their eyes and hit a caribou, for the sheer number of the herd was enormous. Both men fired off shots and three caribou dropped to the ground.

Eli was about to shoot again when Curly Bill stopped him. "That's enough. We only kill what we need to survive." Later that night after they had gutted and skinned the caribou, the men sat down and had their first meal of fresh meat. They felt good about their hunting experience. Each man skinned the hides off the caribou and created a winter coat which doubled as a blanket at night. The fur kept the men warm during the cold Canadian nights.

Chapter 22:

As time went on, the men were able to finish the addition to Curly Bill's cabin. They waterproofed the roof with pine boughs and went down to the river to gather large stones to create a fireplace in their cabin. When the men stood back to admire their handiwork, they were both pleased at how well the cabin looked. The cabin itself now had a beautiful stone fireplace with a chimney going out the roof, a set of bunk beds where the men slept, and a small kitchen with a giant wooden table to skin the animals they would trap. Outside the cabin they built a cache (a wooden structure on stilts) in which they ran a ladder up to it where they put the caribou meat. This method of storage prevented their food from attracting hungry animals looking for food. A corral was also built for the horses and mule out of popular trees.

That night, a small fire was made inside of the fireplace. Snow was falling, and the wolves outside were howling. The temperature had fallen to five degrees, but the cabin stayed warm because of the warmth the fire emitted. The men were admiring how nice it was to have a cabin big enough for the two of them when they heard their horses starting to stir outside.

"Hee haw, hee haw!" the old mule started to bray loudly outside. The men got up to investigate just as they heard the sound of their horses' hoof beats galloping away. Both men grabbed their six-shooters and rushed out of the door. As Curly Bill reached the porch, he could see the horses disappearing into the woods led away by three Indian braves.

"Eli, get out here!"

As Eli reached the porch, he could only see the tails of the horses and the feathers sticking out of the Indian braves' headbands as they disappeared into the woods.

"They stole our horses!"

Chapter 23:

Eli and Curly Bill stood outside, helplessly watching their only mode of transportation disappear into the woods. Both men had their six-shooters drawn, but it was impossible to shoot and not hit the horses. They put their weapons back into their holsters in disbelief. An eerie silence surrounded them as they stood in the falling snow. As they turned to go back inside, something jumped from the roof.

"Ahhjjjhhhhh!" With a deafening battle cry, two Indian braves landed just in front of Eli and Curly Bill. Before the two men could react, two large spears were thrust up to their necks. The braves, covered in war paint, looked at the men with burning hate in their eyes. Curly Bill reached for his six-shooter but was hit in the stomach with a large, blunt club. As he fell to the ground, he saw Eli take the same blows and fall to the ground next to him.

Both men slowly got back to their feet, keeping their hands over their faces to prevent another blow, this time to the head. As they got to their feet, they looked around, but there was no one there. The Indians had disappeared as quietly as they had come. Eli and Curly Bill stood ready for another attack, shaking with fear.

After a couple of tense moments, Curly Bill remarked, "They could have killed us if they wanted to. I believe they were warning us."

"What do you mean they were warning us?" Eli asked.

"The attack was their way of telling us that we are trespassing on their hunting land."

"Well, if they wanted us to leave, why did they steal our horses?"

"They want us to leave, but they don't want us to make it out alive. This land is prime for trapping. They believe if we make it out of here alive, we'll bring back more men and guns and take this land for ourselves. The furs a man can collect from the animals in these parts can bring a fortune, and the Indians want to prevent that from happening."

Chapter 24:

As the men went back into the cabin, they made sure the board on the back of the door was firmly in place to keep intruders out. They washed their wounds and prepared to go to bed. As he loaded his pistol with bullets, Curly Bill remarked, "Eli, I hope you don't do any sleep walking tonight, because if you do I'm liable to fill you with some lead." Eli laughed at that and reassured Curly Bill that he was exhausted and planned on going right to sleep.

During the middle of the night, Eli was jolted awake by a sound coming from the front door of the cabin. Eli, now fully awake, reached for his six-shooter as the door started to shake violently.

"Curly Bill, Curly Bill, wake up," Eli whispered.

"What...What do you want, Eli," Curly Bill asked groggily.

Suddenly Curly Bill heard the noise too. The men had their eyes trained on the door when the blade of a knife came through the casing surrounding the door and lifted the safety board. Curly Bill flipped the mattress he was sleeping on over for protection, and the men took position behind it. At that moment, the log fell from the door and it started to inch open.

Chapter 25:

Curly Bill and Eli cocked the hammers on their six-shooters and their fingers started to pull back on the triggers when the door was kicked opened and a familiar voice rang out, "Hey, hey, howdy, boys!" It was Miner Mike. "Hee hee hee, did I startle ya? Man, I...I...I'm a thirsty. Do you boys have any coffee on?"

Eli and Curly Bill stood there dumbfounded with their mouths hanging wide open. They watched as Miner Mike and his mule Sal walked right into their cabin. As Miner Mike strolled into their kitchen, he looked around admiring their handiwork.

"Hey, boys, you got that coffee yet?" Miner Mike asked as chewing tobacco juice sprayed out from his toothless gums. "We're pretty hun...hung...hungry, yeah that's the word. Oh, and Sal likes her coffee with a pinch a sugar in it."

Curly Bill had seen enough. "Get that mule out of here."

Miner Mike reacted, "Well, where I go Sal goes too."

"Well, you can leave too," Curly Bill said, not knowing who the old man was.

Miner Mike said, looking straight at Eli, "I...I...I thought a man could get a little more respect after saving your life."

Eli immediately put his hand on Miner Mike's shoulder and said, "Forgive my friend here. We've had an eventful night. Curly Bill, I'd like you to meet Miner Mike."

Chapter 26:

Eli went and got Miner Mike a chair and everyone sat down at the table. Before Eli could sit in his chair, he saw Sal back up and sit down at the table like she was one of the men. As he looked closer at Sal, he noticed that she had a big wad of chewing tobacco in her lip! That old mule was chewing tobacco. Eli waited for her to spit, but she never did. So there sat Sal and Miner Mike, each wolfing down leftover salad and sipping their coffee as if nothing was wrong.

After the man and mule had finished their meal, Miner Mike said to Curly Bill, "Looking at the way Sal is acting, I reckon you better open the door and let her out."

Curly Bill opened the door and let Sal out, and the men sat back down at the table and started to talk. Miner Mike started, "The Indians have your horses, huh?"

Curly Bill, surprised at that comment, asked, "How did you know that?"

Miner Mike finished the last of his coffee and said, "I sat up on that hill beyond your cabin and watched the whole thing. It... It was a good show! Sal and I watched as the Indians cut the ropes holding your horses, and...and...um...then you men came out of your cabins looking like fools, totally unaware, yup, unaware, that the Indians were right above you. But I knew, yeah, I knew, I knew they weren't gonna hurt you. You see, they was just warning you that this is their land. You see, I know these Indians well, and um, they don't like you. But..but…but from what I understand, yup, what I understand, they're going to move their tribe for the winter. So good…good…good possibility you can stay here for the winter. But be careful not to stay too long because they'll be comin' back when—"

Before Miner Mike could finish his sentence the clanging of pots and pans could be heard outside the cabin. Realizing that Sal had taken off again, Miner Mike got up from his chair and opened the cabin door and yelled, "You get back here, you no good flea-mangled mule, right this moment!" And before the men could say good-bye, Miner Mike was out the door, chasing Sal down the trail.

Chapter 27:

    Many months passed by after the incident with the Indians. The men decided on staying for the time being and trapping the Canadian wilderness as they had originally planned. There had been no sightings of the Indians, so the men assumed that the information Miner Mike had given them was true. Eli and Curly Bill mapped out a plan for laying their traps, and under Curly Bill's direction, Eli became a very efficient trapper.

    Eli and Curly Bill's trap line ran in a giant circle around their cabin. They set many traps around the circle, and at the start of each week they would each go their own way around the circle to check the traps for animals. They would set out on a Monday and it would take several days to check the traps before they met back at the cabin to skin the animals they caught. The men built toboggan-like sleds to carry all of the furs they caught in their traps back to the cabin.

    Along Eli's trap line ran a wide river that dead-ended into a beaver pond. Beaver pelts in those days had a high value on the market and proved fairly easy to trap. Now beavers build walk-ways across the water called dams using tree branches and other shrubbery. The dam causes water on one side to become high, and on the other side of the dam it lowers. If a part of the dam breaks and water rushes over, the beavers immediately begin repairing the leak in order to prevent the water level from dropping.

Along with building a dam, beavers also construct their own living quarters, referred to as a lodge. Each lodge has an underwater passageway leading up to a mound where the beavers sleep, store food, and keep their young. Beavers also store tree branches on the muddy bottom of the pond so that in the winter they can take these branches up into their lodge and eat them when food becomes scarce. The white snow that falls in the winter makes the shiny reddish- brown coat of the beaver easy to spot for predators looking for their next meal, so beavers stay underneath the ice for the majority of the winter.

It was late October when the ice began to freeze over on the beaver pond. The men were starting to catch a lot of furs but had to carry all of the animals on their toboggans because the Indians had stolen their horses and mule. It took a considerable amount of time for the men to complete the process. The colder the Canadian winter got, the thicker the animals' fur became, which increased the amount of coins the men would receive.

Eli was two days into checking his trap line when he had arrived at the beaver pond. Whenever he came to the pond, he would walk on top of the dam to get to the beaver lodge. Once he arrived at the lodge, he would carefully pull away the sticks that covered the beavers' chamber and set a trap. Knowing their lodge had been disturbed the beavers would repair the damages and become ensnared in the trap Eli set.

When the beavers got caught in the trap they were ensnared with a wire. When they dove into the water to get away from the trap, the weight of the trap caused them to drown. This method was usually more humane than other methods of trapping because the beaver usually died right away. Other trapping methods caused the animal to become ensnared in the trap and then wait in the bitter cold for the owner of the trap to come back and club it to death.

As Eli worked on setting the trap inside the beaver lodge, the sound of the water rushing past him meant he could not 🐾 hear very well. But he had just set his trap and was admiring the looks of it when he heard a faint cracking noise from the dam behind him. Eli's first reaction was to take a moment to formulate a plan. After living in the dangerous woodlands of Canada for some time now, Eli had learned that it was better to think first and respond later. After taking a deep breath, Eli slowly reached for his six-shooter. He was careful not to drop the gun in the water, for his hands had begun to shake violently with fear.

By now whatever was approaching behind him on the dam was within striking distance. Eli froze as he felt heavy breathing on his neck while his nostrils were repulsed by a strong odor. Eli quickly turned only to come face to face with a massive one-eyed grizzly bear!

Chapter 28:

The bear stood on all four paws as it slowly smelled the air around Eli. Eli tried to remain as still as possible, hoping the bear's naturally poor eyesight would cause the bear to lose interest in him. The bear sniffed the air a few more times before turning around and walking toward the open beaver lodge. Eli let out a silent breath of relief and turned to flee, but his leg had grown numb and fallen asleep, causing him to suddenly stumble backwards on the dam. Crack! A branch underneath Eli's foot snapped, drawing the attention of the grizzly bear. The bear reared around and charged in Eli's direction.

Immediately Eli grabbed his six-shooter from his holster in order to shoot the bear, but his sudden movement caused the bear to become startled and swat Eli across the face with its massive paw. Eli went sprawling backwards into the freezing water. As Eli descended into the depths of the cold water, he realized that the bear would be waiting for him to surface. A bear that did not hibernate in the winter only meant one thing: it was starving and looking for food!

Eli began to panic until he remembered a story Curly Bill had once told him about a pond that had dried up during a drought, causing a beaver lodge to become stranded without water. Curly Bill said that grown men were able to poke their heads up into the beaver house and look around. This beaver lodge was bigger than any lodge Eli had ever seen before, and he knew that there was a chance that if he swam up one of the underwater passageways he could hide from the bear in the lodge.

Chapter 29:

Eli began swimming toward one of the tunnels leading up into the lodge. The water was murky, making it hard to judge if the tunnel was big enough for him to swim up into. When Eli reached the tunnel, he thrust his body toward the opening of the lodge, but to his dismay he became stuck. As he looked up, he could see the surface of the water inches above his head. Eli could not seem to gather the leverage needed to pull himself up into the lodge. His lungs were starting to ache as he slowly suffocated because of the lack of air. He reached desperately into the lodge, hoping to find an object to pull himself up with. As he searched, his hand came into contact with a branch sticking out of the side of the wall. Using the last bit of strength he could muster, Eli pulled himself into the lodge.

Eli collapsed onto the mound of mud, gasping for air. For a brief moment, Eli could rest easy, but that luxury was taken away as the bear became aware that Eli was no longer in the water. The bear climbed on top of the lodge and began tearing into the beaver house after him. Eli would crawl to a different part of the lodge after each swipe of the grizzly bear's paw.

After several failed attempts, the bear began to track Eli by sniffing into the breathing tubes sticking out of the top of the lodge. After sniffing around, the grizzly located where Eli was and used its three-inch claws to rip apart the beaver house. Every time the bear clawed a hole into the roof, it would stick its big old snout into the hole and sniff out where Eli had moved to.

By now Eli had gathered his strength back, and he took his six-shooter and stuck it up into one of the holes the bear had made and prepared to unload several bullets into the skull of that grizzly bear. He waited until the bear stuck its nose in the hole and he pulled the trigger—click!

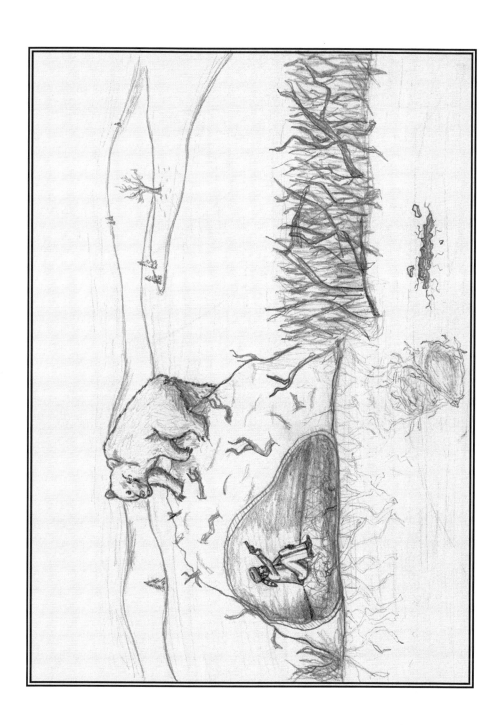

Chapter 30:

Eli panicking realized that his ammunition had become wet from his swim and the gun had been rendered useless. Eli now had to make a decision between two choices: stay in the beaver house and fight the grizzly, or risk diving back into the freezing water and try to swim to safety. As he debated the dilemma, a beaver popped up through the tunnel next to Eli. As he stared at the beaver, he wondered how it could stay underwater without coming to the surface for air. By now the grizzly was inches away from tearing the top off of the lodge, frightening the beaver, which dove back into the water. Eli, seeing no other solution at the time, took a deep breath and dove into the water after the beaver.

The water was frigid. Eli had planned to swim down past where the bear was and crawl out on the dam behind the bear, but he soon realized he could not hold his breath long enough to get a safe distance from the bear.

He had started to panic as his lungs ached for air when he witnessed the beaver swimming up to the ice. It put its mouth to the ice, breathed in, and swam away as if it had gone to the surface. Eli realized there were air pockets on the bottom surface of the ice!

Eli swam up to an air pocket on the ice and breathed a fresh breath of air. Eli could see the bear tearing into the beaver house every time he went to the surface to breathe in the air bubbles on the bottom of the ice. He repeatedly swam to the surface, breathed, and continued swimming until he was a safe distance away from the bear. He reached up and broke through the ice and crawled out of the water. The bear stayed occupied with the beaver house as Eli tiptoed to the end of the dam. With one last look over his shoulder, Eli took off toward the cabin.

Eli ran until he could not run anymore. As he stopped to catch his breath, he realized that he now faced a new danger: his clothes were starting to freeze on him! As quickly as he could, Eli stripped out of all his clothes and laid them in the snow. He pushed snow on top of his clothing until they became as stiff as a board, and then he crumpled them up and beat them against a tree. As Eli beat his pants against the tree the ice fell from his clothes and they became dry again. Eli was thankful that he had stayed up on those long winter nights listening to Curly Bill's survival tips. They had saved his life twice in the same day.

Chapter 31:

Eli was still a long way from his cabin, and he knew that if he did not make it back to the cabin by nightfall, he would freeze to death in the cold. It started to snow lightly, making it hard to follow the trail. He searched for familiar landmarks to guide him. Looking around he found something that chilled his body to the bone: fresh pony tracks!

The Indians had returned! It looked to Eli to be about four or five horses. There was no time to sit and stare at the tracks, for Eli's body was starting to tingle as frostbite started to set in.

As thoughts swirled through his mind, Eli picked up the smell of smoke and knew that he was close to the cabin. He saw the many stumps Curly Bill had cut to construct their cabin and his pace quickened. After a few more steps he broke free of the woods and came into the clearing where the cabin sat. He broke into a sprint and flung open the door expecting to see Curly Bill inside. But the fire in the fireplace was dying out.

Eli stoked the fire until it burned brightly and huddled up next to the warmth, trying to regain his body temperature. He collapsed in pure exhaustion due to the day's events next to the fire but was awakened by a knock on the door. The log across the door started to rattle. Eli immediately sat straight up. As the noise continued, Eli reached for his six-shooter, and when his hand grasped the handle of the pistol, his heart sank; he had forgot to replace his wet ammunition from the beaver dam experience! His gun would be useless against the intruder.

Chapter 32:

Someone started pounding hard on the door, causing the log to rattle even more. Eli searched for a place to hide from the intruder when a voice rang out from behind the door, "Eli, let me in!" It was Curly Bill! Overcome with relief that Curly Bill had not been captured by the Indians, Eli raced to the door and let him in.

Curly Bill burst through the door and the two men started telling each other about the eventful day they had. After Eli told Curly Bill about the bear, Curly Bill said, "On my way back I walked by that dam, and I saw the destruction that was left and the bear tracks leading up to it, and I didn't expect to find you here. Let me tell you something, buddy, I'm glad to see you alive." Eli had been around Curly Bill for a long time, but this was the first time he had ever seen him this emotional. After a long pause, Curly Bill said, "Well, I'm hungry, do you have anything cooking?"

The two men laughed. Eli said, "No, I haven't been here that long. Curly Bill, I got some bad news, I saw pony tracks on my hike back!"

Curly Bill, with fear in his eyes, responded, "I know, I saw them too."

Eli gasped, "You did? How many were there?"

"Six braves, dressed in their war clothes, their faces painted."

Eli started to panic. "What do you think they were doing?"

"I think they're after us."

"Well, what are we going to do? Let's get out of here. We got enough fur to buy us a cabin somewhere else."

"No," Curly Bill said sternly, "we've been here too long. It's snowing heavily right now and it'll probably keep them from doing anything tonight. Let's spend the night and pack up tomorrow morning."

Eli agreed and the men sat staring into the fire. Both men's faces bore the strain of worry, because they knew the fate that many trappers had experienced at the hand of Indians.

"Eli, we have to stay alert tonight just in case they come," Curly Bill said.

"I agree," Eli said more confidently. "I'll take the first watch and we'll rotate every two hours."

The men went outside to do a walk around the cabin before Curly Bill went to sleep. They were amazed to find that it had snowed almost a foot while they were inside. After they had stoked the fire one last time, Curly Bill went to his bunk and Eli sat down in his chair. Five minutes went by and Eli could hear Curly Bill snoring loudly. The snoring was so loud that Eli threw objects he found around the cabin at Curly Bill to try and get him to stop. As the snoring ceased, Eli was left alone with his thoughts. But Eli had a weakness for warm fires and he soon fell asleep.

Chapter 33:

Around three o'clock in the morning a strange noise woke Eli from his slumber. After listening for a few moments, Eli decided that it must have been Curly Bill snoring in his sleep, so he laid his head back on his pillow. The silence in the room was deafening, and Eli was about to rise and get Curly Bill up to take the next shift when he heard the noise again. The noise was coming from the roof!

"Curly Bill, Curly Bill!"

Curly Bill sat up, confused. "What's the matter?"

"Shhh, listen."

Curly Bill's eyes grew big when he heard the sound. He slowly eased off his bunk next to Eli.

"What do you think it is?" Eli asked.

Curly Bill's response chilled Eli to the bone. "Indians."

At the same time the two men realized that the smoke from their fire was no longer going up the chimney. Smoke started to fill the room, causing the men to cough.

"The Indians are on the roof and they've put an animal hide over the chimney in order to smoke us out. As soon as we walk out of here, they're going to spear us," Curly Bill yelled.

In a panic and coughing hard, Eli said, "What are we going to do?"

"Don't panic." Curly Bill could see Eli needed to get out of the smoke as soon as possible. "Think now, does your pistol work?"

"Yes, I dried my bullets."

"Do you have your rifle and knife?"

"Yes, I have both."

"I've got the same, now follow me."

Chapter 34:

The smoke had almost completely filled the cabin so the two men got on their hands and knees to avoid it. As they crawled, Curly Bill turned to Eli and said, "They're going to be waiting for us to burst through the door and then they'll attack us, but we're going to surprise them. We're going to open the door and run out there with our guns blazing at the first sign of anything that moves."

Eli took out his bowie knife and put it between his teeth and grabbed a six-shooter and his rifle in each of his hands. The men were determined not to die without a fight. Curly Bill was the first to move. He took the log from the door and with a determined look on his face mouthed the words "Good Luck" to Eli. He turned and opened the door.

Both men burst out of the door looking to fire on whatever occupied the roof. As their eyes searched frantically for foes, they realized no one was outside. They studied their surroundings; all they could see was fresh snow around them, but no tracks of any kind. Smoke was now billowing out of the cabin because there was so much of it.

Eli turned to Curly Bill and muttered, "What's going on? I don't understand."

Curly Bill responded, "Let's walk around the cabin and look for tracks. Whatever was on our roof had to have left some kind of print." And then he stopped and turned around. "Hey, what if it was just an animal that was crawling around by the chimney searching for a warm place to sleep? If it got caught in the chimney, then it would have caused the smoke to come into our cabin."

The men started to chuckle at their foolishness. They decided to walk around the cabin just to be sure. Before they took off, the men sat back to admire how beautiful the freshly fallen snow looked under the Canadian stars. As the men stared, Eli thought he saw little holes in the snow about five feet to his left.

"Curly Bill, look at the little holes in the snow. What do you reckon those are?"

Curly Bill turned and looked at the holes in the snow and said, "I don't know, I've never seen anything like that before."

The night around them was still, the air chilly to the touch, and the moon was casting an eerie shadow around them.

"Wait a minute," said Eli, "it almost seems as if steam is coming up from the snow." Eli took a step toward the hole to investigate the cause of the steam when Curly Bill yelled, "Eli, wait!!"

Chapter 35:

It was too late; up from the snow rose six Indian braves with massive spears. They had been lying on the ground for hours as the snow fell on top of them. Their breath had created the holes that Eli had seen. The braves let out a piercing war cry as they surrounded the terrified men. Eli turned to run but tripped, and two braves jumped on top of him, holding a razor-sharp spear inches from his face. Eli turned to see his burly six-foot-three-inch comrade stumbling around with three braves hanging from his body. Eli turned back to face his assailants just in time to see the butt of the spear come down on his head.

Chapter 36:

Eli awoke to find himself tied back to back with Curly Bill securely to a pole in the center of a tepee. He reckoned that it was early in the morning because the sun had not yet come up. It was very dark inside the tepee and it took a minute for Eli's eyes to adjust to the darkness. As he struggled against the rope that held him to the pole, he heard the sound of drum beats and people's feet stomping to the beat as they cried, "HiyaaHiyaaHiyaayayay." The pounding of the drums matched the pounding in Eli's head as he groggily came to. Eli could feel Curly Bill struggle against the ropes, but as powerful as he was, he was no match for the strength of the rope.

"Curly Bill, where are we?"

"I believe we're in their village."

"What are they going to do with us?" Eli asked nervously.

"I don't know. I've got to think," responded Curly Bill.

The men sat struggling to get their hands free.

Curly Bill encouraged Eli, "Just keep working on it."

"I am, but the ropes are cutting into my wrists, I can feel my wrists bleeding."

"So what," grunted Curly Bill. "There'll be more blood coming if we don't get out of here."

"Do you think they'll scalp us?" asked Eli nervously.

"Most likely. These men are savages, not a shred of mercy in them."

That knowledge made Eli work harder at getting free from the ropes. Soon the tempo of the music started to die down and the noise outside of the tepee started to settle. Every now and then the sound of a dog barking off into the distance could be heard, but the silence was starting to get to the two men.

"Why did they stop?" asked Eli.

"I don't know."

"Do you think they'll come for us?"

"I don't know that either. If the flap on the tepee opens then you'll know."

The men continued to work on the ropes around their wrists when Curly Bill heard footsteps approaching the tepee. Curly Bill's heart started to race within his chest.

"Eli, brace yourself, they're coming for us."

The men worked so hard at getting the ropes off that blood started pouring from their wrists. As the men collapsed in exhaustion, the tepee flap opened.

Chapter 37:

Both men strained their eyes to see who the shadowy figure was. The only sound that could be heard was the men's hearts beating wildly. The figure in the doorway reached into a bag hanging from his neck and pulled out a lantern. When the lantern was lit, the light revealed the smiling outline of an old toothless man.

"Hee hee! How ya doing, boys!" Eli and Curly Bill could not believe their eyes.

Miner Mike, who seemed to be enjoying the moment, sat back with a big old toothless grin and laughed. "Hee hee! Here I am again, boys. I've come to save...save you." Miner Mike reached into his saddle bag again and pulled out his bowie knife and cut the ropes that held the men. The men instantly were on their feet, rubbing their swollen wrists. Miner Mike was quick to say, "You ... You better be quiet. Yup, yup, quiet indeed, because you know what, I think they want to eat you."

The men's faces turned white. "Hee hee, I'm just pullin' your leg, but I know they...they... want to scal...scal...scalp you because they ain't happy with you...you disobeying their orders. I've been waitin'...outside in the cold for them to go to bed so I could ...could rescue you. Isn't it funny how I'm always saving you?"

After listening to Miner Mike ramble on, Eli interrupted him, "Hey, where's Sal?"

Curly Bill slapped Eli on the back of the head. "You were just saved from certain death and you're worrying about a mule?"

"Well, yeah, I don't want her waking the Indians up with those pots and pans banging around."

Miner Mike looked at the two men and said, "Oh yeah, I didn't think...think about that."

Sure enough the men heard the sound of pots and pan clanging together as Sal was going tepee to tepee searching for Miner Mike. The dogs in the village started to bark and the camp began to stir. Miner Mike grinned. "Well, sorry, boys, but you're ...you're on your own." And with that Miner Mike grabbed Sal by the reins and took off for the brush.

Chapter 38:

By now the entire village was awake. Two braves mounted their ponies and rushed into the brush after Miner Mike. Curly Bill and Eli slowly snuck out of the tepee and, once out, made a break for the woods. The men ran as fast as they could. They could hear the dogs barking behind them as they tracked them, and behind the dogs came the sound of galloping horses coming up fast. Curly Bill knew that if they could just make it to the river they could jump in and the sweeping current would take them downstream faster than the braves could ride through the thick brush.

"Eli, run for the river, run for the river!"

Eli changed directions and made a beeline for the river, which was now in view. Both men could feel the breath of the dogs upon their heels and hear the whooping of the braves in hot pursuit.

The men were within ten feet of the river when one of the dogs lunged and bit down on Eli's pant leg, pulling him to the ground. Curly Bill stopped to help his friend, but Eli pushed him away. "Save yourself, Curly Bill!"

At that moment, an arrow flew in and snagged Eli in the shoulder. Curly Bill, refusing to leave, tried to pull the dog off of Eli. Before he could, an enormous brave came riding through the brush and draped a net across Curly Bill's body. Curly Bill struggled to get free, but when he finally got the net off of his shoulders he realized they were surrounded. Six braves surrounded the men, bows pulled back with sharp arrows aimed right in his direction. Realizing nothing more could be done, Curly Bill threw up his hands in surrender.

Chapter 39:

The Indian braves led the men back to the village. The braves had tied the hands of Curly Bill in front of him and had a rope connecting the back of the horse to his neck. Eli had fainted from the loss of blood caused by the arrow in his shoulder, so the braves draped him across the back of a horse. The procession traveling through the village included three braves in front, Curly Bill in the middle, and three braves bringing up the rear. The lead brave stopped in front of a tepee and picked up Eli and carried him inside.

Eli awoke to find himself staring up into the face of a beautiful Indian squaw. She was taller than any woman he had ever seen. Eli noticed that she had beautiful facial features, long black hair, brown eyes, and white, pearly teeth. She had just removed the arrow from Eli's shoulder while he was unconscious and was now placing medicine in the gaping hole left in Eli's shoulder. He nearly passed out again when he witnessed the bloody bandages sitting beside him. The arrow was equipped with barbs at the tip that had pulled bits of flesh off Eli's shoulder when it was removed. Eli looked around for Curly Bill but saw no sign of his friend.

He angrily got up and shouted, "What did you do with my friend?"

Startled, the squaw smiled. *"Haaah, epivah-wuh-ennah."*

"I don't know what you're saying," Eli said, half angry, half transfixed by her beauty.

She tried to talk again, but seeing that Eli did not understand her, she tried another tactic. "You rest now."

Eli could not believe his luck, "You speak English?"

"You rest," the Indian said in a harsher tone.

"Is that all the English you know?" Eli asked.

"No," she responded hesitantly. "Me know more. You rest now."

"Curly Bill's dead, isn't he."

"You rest now," the Indian girl said as she inserted some medicine into Eli's mouth and watched him drift off to sleep.

Chapter 40:

Two days went by before Eli woke up. As he groggily sat up, pain shot up his arm, but as he took off the bandages he could see that the injury was already starting to heal. As he put his bandages back on, the pretty squaw walked into the tepee with a bowl of soup. "You eat bear meat."

She started to spoon feed Eli, who eagerly ate because he hadn't eaten in three days. When he had finished eating, he motioned for something to drink.

"You want water?"

This response stunned Eli and he assumed that she knew more English than she let on.

"I want to ask you now," Eli said sheepishly, "please tell me where my friend Curly Bill is."

Without answering him the squaw took the bowl and went out of the tepee, but before she left, Eli caught her looking back at him. They both blushed.

Another night passed as Eli tried to drum up the strength to make his escape. He had not seen the squaw since their last encounter and he hoped the footsteps he heard walking toward the tepee flap were hers. Unfortunately, when the flap opened, it revealed the enormous frame of the lead brave that had captured him. The brave had war paint under his eyes, a deerskin breech-cloth, and was carrying a long knife in one hand. The brave went behind him and cut the ropes that bound Eli's hands.

"Where are you taking me?" asked Eli. The brave merely grunted and grabbed Eli by the shoulder and pushed him out the door.

Chapter 41:

The brave led Eli up a hill toward the largest tepee in the village. All around the two men children were playing, but as the men passed they stopped their games and stared. It was almost as if Eli was a ghost to them. This tepee had two entrance flaps that were already opened with two braves guarding the entrance. The lead brave pushed Eli through the flap and onto the ground. It took time for Eli's eyes to adjust to the darkness inside the tepee, but he could hear the voices of others in the tepee with him. When his eyes finally adjusted, he noticed another man lying on the floor next to him, a big curly headed man!

Eli looked over and yelled, "Curly Bill, are you all right?" An Indian brave walked over to Eli and kicked him in the stomach. Eli doubled over in pain, but the brave would not let him sulk. The brave immediately pulled Eli and Curly Bill up by their hair and made them kneel in front of an old man with an enormous eagle-feathered headdress, the tribal chief.

The chief sat with his arms crossed, a scowl on his face, countless scars adorning his head and body. He had long black hair that was braided into ponytails that hung past his shoulders, a bear claw necklace, and moccasins that came up to his knees. He was a powerful-looking man with three Indian braves on either side of his seat.

Eli glanced toward the flap, but there would be no escaping, for an angry-looking brave guarded the door. Curly Bill tried to speak but was immediately silenced with a hand across the face by one of the braves guarding the chief. The tribal leader unfolded his arms, put his hands on his knees, and began to speak, *"Ga-do-a-na-du-ne."*

Eli and Curly Bill could not understand what the chief was saying but then, to their surprise, the chief said, "Why have you come?"

Eli rose up to speak and the brave moved to slap him, so Eli immediately dropped back to his knees. The chief began to speak again. "You men, we warned you. You come to our land, you kill our animals, you steal our fur, you cut our trees down. What right do you have to do this?"

Curly Bill responded, "Sir, we came to trap. We meant you no harm."

The chief raised his hand and cut Curly Bill off. "Me no hear now. You wonder why I speak English. White missionaries come long time past. They tell us about your God, we believe your God, our God, is great God. But other white men come and kill our people, push us off our land, they drive us to these lands, and now you come and push us further. Your people, they kill my son, they shed his blood. My people think I should shed your blood now, but because I serve God of mercy I will give you one more chance. You leave this country and never return."

Chapter 42:

As soon as the chief stopped speaking a brave pulled out a knife and came toward Eli. Eli jumped up, not wanting to lose his scalp, and raced backwards, but his hands were tied. The brave kicked Eli to the floor with a deadening thud and cut the ropes from his hands. Curly Bill, knowing better, offered up his hands and the brave cut his ropes. When the ropes came off of Curly Bill's wrists, they left deep wounds because the Indians were known for dipping leather strips in water and tying there prisoners hands with the straps. As the leather dried, it would slowly shrink, embedding itself in the prisoner's skin.

The chief sat back in his chair, his arms crossed. Four braves descended around Eli and Curly Bill and led them outside the tepee. The lead brave pointed toward the direction of their cabin and grunted. As they made their way out of the village, the children ran out to them laughing and pointing as they tried to touch them to make sure they were real.

As the men passed by the tent in which the beautiful squaw lived, Eli stopped. "Curly Bill, you go on to where the river meets the trail. I'll meet you there, but I have to do something first."

Curly Bill, seeing that Eli wore the same smile he had on at the saloon when he had kissed Millie, said, "Now don't make any more trouble for us. If they catch you, you're on your own."

Eli laughed, picked up an Osoberry flower that had sprouted through the snow, and disappeared into the tepee.

Chapter 43:

The squaw jumped up immediately when Eli walked into the tepee. "Please, don't be scared," said Eli as he took off his cowboy hat to show he meant no harm. "My name is Eli Johnson."

The Indian girl breathed a sigh of relief and sheepishly said, "Me Sparrow."

Eli extended the flower toward Sparrow and said, "The chief says we have to go. Please take this flower to remember me by."

And with that Eli reached in and gave her a kiss on the cheek. As Eli turned to leave he heard Sparrow say with a giggle, "I hope to see you again, Eli Johnson." Surprised, Eli turned and tipped his hat and winked as he disappeared through the flap of the tepee.

Eli met up with Curly Bill and they followed the river for miles. Curly Bill knew the forest well and the men reached their cabin by nightfall. The men were overjoyed when they returned home and saw that the Indians had returned their horses. Eli rushed over to Scout and threw his arms around him, thankful that he did not have to suffer the loss of another companion. The men went inside and built a fire and contemplated their next move.

"We have to get out of Canada right away," said Eli as he packed his belongings.

"No, not yet," Curly Bill said as he stared into the roaring fire.

"What do you mean no? The Indians…if we stay, they won't give us anymore chances."

"We have to pull our traps and then get out of here. Without the money those furs will bring, our entire stay in Canada will be in vain. Tomorrow morning we'll check our trap-line. You go your way and I'll go down mine." With that, Curly Bill put his hat over his eyes and fell asleep, but Eli continued to stare into the fire. He did not have a good feeling about this plan.

Chapter 44:

Early the next morning the men gathered their traps and met back at the cabin. They took time to carefully close down the cabin in case they were ever able to come back to it. Then the men carefully skinned the animals they had trapped so that they would not take up room in their saddlebags. As Curly Bill loaded the last of the men's possessions on the horses, something moved in the bushes behind them. "Did you hear that, Curly Bill?"

"Yes, it came from over there in the bushes, right by the sugar maple tr—"

Wham! An arrow went right through Curly Bill's hat, pinning it to the tree behind him. "Eli, we're under attack, run!"

Curly Bill and Eli jumped on their horses and took off toward the trail as arrows hit everywhere around them. When they reached the edge of the woods, Eli stopped. "We forgot the saddlebag with the mink furs in it! Those furs are worth more than all the others combined! I'm going back for them."

"It's too late," said Curly Bill with fear in his eyes, "you'll never survive."

But Eli was determined to get them back. Eli dug his spurs into Scout and off they went.

Eli remembered the furs were in the sleeping area of the cabin. *I'll just sneak in the back window,* thought Eli. Eli left Scout by a tree and climbed through the window. As he reached for the bag of furs, the butt of a spear hit him in the back. Eli crumpled to the floor. Eli rolled onto his back to stare up into the eyes of the lead brave from the Indian village standing above him with a spear, waiting to plunge it down into Eli.

"Wait, Bear Claw!" Both men turned to see Sparrow running toward them. "Please, spare him."

"You know I cannot. Chief has given order to kill man because he take furs after final warning."

"But I love Eli Johnson," Sparrow said with tears in her eyes.

Bear Claw looked down at Eli and then back at Sparrow. "I let man live if you be my wife."

"No, Sparrow!" Eli yelled, trying to get up. "Don't do—" Eli was knocked back to the floor by Bear Claw's spear.

"You make decision now, or I kill your Eli.

Sparrow looked at Eli and then back to Bear Claw. "I will be your wife."

Bear Claw took Eli's gun from his holster and led him by spear point to the window. "You run now and never return."

Eli was shoved out the window and nearly fell on top of Curly Bill, who had circled back to help Eli. "I must save her," Eli said.

"No," Curly Bill said sternly. "She made a decision to save your life. If you let the other Indians see that Bear Claw let you go, they'll kill Sparrow and Bear Claw for disobeying the chief's orders. Besides, what kind of life could you give her, a life on the run? She belongs here, with her people."

Eli was about to refuse when an Indian brave came around the corner and saw the men. The brave yipped to sound the alarm that he had found the men. Seeing no way to change the situation, Eli nodded to Curly Bill and the men jumped on their horses and ran for the woods as arrows flew around them.

As they reached the forest edge, Eli turned to Curly Bill and said, "Where should we go now?"

"I know a little town in the Colorado mountains where you can get a mint for animal furs," Curly Bill said with a chuckle.

A smile crossed Eli's face. "Dustbowl here we come. Yeehaw!"

Made in the USA
Charleston, SC
13 April 2011